The Australian ABC

Written by Colin Thiele

hinkler

One day a call went out across Australia,
To forests, deserts, creeks and city fountains,
For animals to leave their homes and hollows
To hold a special meeting in the mountains.
They came in every weather, fine or wet,
Until their names used up the alphabet.

A ANT answered quickly, scrambling so we're told
Down bright ACACIA blossoms touched with gold.

B BILBY came next, pad-padding in the hush,
Past BANKSIA heads that some call bottlebrush.

CROCODILE lumbered past the COOLABAHS
Her eyes at night as bright as shining stars.

DINGO loped leanly with sunlight on his back
Past DESERT PEAS of brilliant red and black.

ECHIDNA walked with prickles in his pants
And probed the EUCALYPTUS for nesting ants.

F FROGMOUTH flew forward with a funny grin,
A tuft of FEATHER FLOWERS at her chin.

GOANNA rattled up the mountainside
Scattering the fallen GUMNUTS in his stride.

HERON flapped slowly from her sandy bay,
HIBISCUS flowers pointing out the way.

IBIS stopped prodding with his sickle beak
Where straggling IRONBARKS lined the reedy creek.

Beyond the JERRY-JERRY bushes JABIRU
Ended his dance and joined the travellers too.

K KOALA was shaken from her midday snooze
When KANGAROO PAWS showed her the route to choose.

LYREBIRD spread his tail for all to see,
Not even LILIES were as beautiful as he.

M MAGPIE gloried in his morning song
And left his MULGA tree to join the throng.

NUMBAT with stripes and long impressive tail
Scuttled past NETTLES on the winding trail.

OWL left his barn and ponderously flew
Over the forests where ORCHIDS grew.

P PLATYPUS burrowed from her river bank
Where PAPERBARK saplings gently bent and drank.

Q QUOKKA ate QUANDONGS on his lonely trip
But they were sour and left him with the pip.

R ROSELLA, red and crimson, swooped and swung
As if from REDGUMS loops of fire were hung.

Black SWAN came too, to join the trekking mass,
Past woodlands rich with fragrant SASSAFRAS.

T TURTLE departed from his seaside bank
And trampled the TURKEY BUSHES like a tank.

U No one could match ULYSSES BUTTERFLY
Flitting between UMBRELLA TREE and sky.

V And VELVET RAT, fur-coated in the wet,
slipped slyly off through clumps of VIOLET.

WOMBAT found WARATAHS the way he came,
Marking the path with chalices of flame.

X The shining XMAS BEETLE joined the push
From the branches of a lively XMAS BUSH.

And YELLOW-FOOTED WALLABY climbed the hill
Past spears of YACCAS standing stiff and still.

Then ZEBRA FINCH, perched on a ZAMIA PALM,
Called on the multitude for peace and calm.

They made Goanna chairman. Out he ran
And cleared his throat ~
                    and the conference began.

Glossary

Acacia
The botanical name for trees and shrubs commonly known as wattle.

Coolabah
An Aboriginal name commonly used for a particular type of eucalyptus or gum tree often found in the Australian inland.
It grows along watercourses and its presence is a sign of water.

Jerry-Jerry
A common name for a small shrub found throughout the Australian bush.

Sassafras
A common name for a family of trees found in the Australian rainforest. Their bark smells strongly of nutmeg.

Yacca
The name given by South Australians to their variety of grasstree.

hinkler

Published by Hinkler Books Pty Ltd
45–55 Fairchild Street
Heatherton Victoria 3202 Australia
www.hinkler.com.au

First published by Weldon Kids Pty Ltd 1992

Illustration and design © Weldon Kids Pty Ltd
Text © Colin Thiele
Cover design © Hinkler Books Pty Ltd 2010

Project coordinator: Leah Walsh
Cover design: Ruth Comey
Prepress: Graphic Print Group

ISBN: 978 1 7418 5287 5

Printed and bound in China

"We would like to dedicate this book to our father, who put the love of books in our veins and taught us that books are our friends, and to our mother, who through her storytelling brought them to life."

~ Leonie and Cecille Weldon ~